For Patrice
D.D.
For Maria
M.E.

First published in the United States by
Ideals Publishing Corporation
Nelson Place at Elm Hill Pike
Nashville, Tennessee 37214

First published in Great Britain by
Piccadilly Press Ltd.
London, England

Printed in Hong Kong by South China Printing Company

Library of Congress Cataloging-in-Publication Data

Day, David. 1947-
    The sleeper / David Day ; illustrated by Mark Entwisle.
        p.   cm.
    Summary: After sleeping in a cave for two hundred years, a young
monk finds that he carries sacred books that can save China in a
time of crisis.
    ISBN 0-8249-8456-0
    [1. Folklore--China.]   I. Entwisle, Mark, 1961-   ill.
II. Title.
PZ8.1.D32S1   1990
398.2--dc20
    [E]   90-30714
                                                                CIP
                                                                 AC

The Sleeper

David Day

ILLUSTRATED BY
Mark Entwisle

IDEALS CHILDREN'S BOOKS
Nashville, Tennessee

High up in the Tong Mountains of China, there lived a boy named Wu Wing Wong of Wulung. His home was the oldest and finest monastery in all the land, and Wu was its youngest monk.

It was a dream come true. Wu had long admired the wise men of the monastery and hoped that one day he, too, might wear the saffron robe of a monk.

But Wu had one big problem: He always slept too late.

Wu Wing Wong could never get enough sleep. No matter how early he went to bed, he just could not wake up in the morning.

When the morning bell sounded over the mountains at dawn, all the other monks awoke, but Wu simply went on sleeping.

Each morning, the monks had to shake Wu and drag him out of bed. Yet despite his sleepy habits, the other monks liked Wu.

"Wu is still a child," one of the elders explained. "He's not lazy. He's just growing and he needs more sleep. We must be patient."

Despite his problem, Wu was happy. He loved reading
and was most contented when surrounded by books.
And the Tong monastery possessed the most magnificent
library in all of China.

But one day, everything changed.

The Emperor, who was called Chin the Merciless, commanded that all the libraries be emptied within 100 days. After that time, only the Emperor would be allowed to own books. And anyone caught with one would be put to death.

The monks had no choice. In just ninety-nine days, their magnificent library had to be emptied. Each day they selected books to be taken away.

On the morning of the ninety-ninth day, the chief librarian called for Wu. Pointing to three packhorses heavily laden with bundles of books and scrolls, the old scholar said, "This is the last of our great library. I left the finest and most important books for last, praying that the Emperor would have a change of heart.

"But no word has come. So now, you must deliver these last books to the Emperor's officers by tomorrow evening."

By midafternoon, Wu saw dark clouds gathering in the sky. He hurried the horses along the forest trail, trying to find shelter before nightfall. But late in the afternoon the rain came pouring down.

The storm grew worse as Wu tried to cross a creek that had flooded into a raging torrent. As he led the horses into the water, there was a roar of thunder and a flash of lightning. At that exact moment, a huge, yellow tiger leaped from a tree onto the back of one of the horses.

All three horses reared back in fear and panic. Both the tiger and Wu were thrown into the water and swept away.

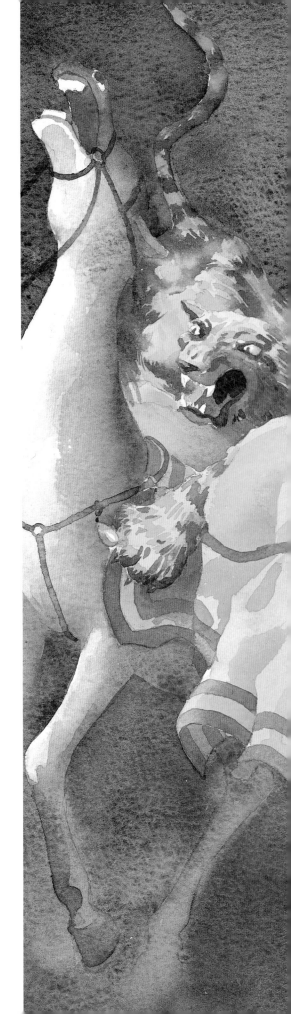

Wu fought to keep his head above the water as he was pulled further and further downstream. Finally, he caught a tree branch. As the tiger whirled by, Wu dragged himself from the creek.

Wiping water from his eyes, Wu struggled to catch sight of the horses. But the animals had fled deep into the woods, and Wu could only follow them by listening for the sound of their hooves. Finally, after a long chase, Wu caught up with the horses where they had come up against the wall of a mountain.

It was dark and the rain still fell. Clutching the horses' reins in his wet fist, Wu gazed at the cliff, hoping to find shelter. Just beyond where they stood, Wu saw a dim light shining from an opening in the cliff wall. It was the mouth of a large cave.

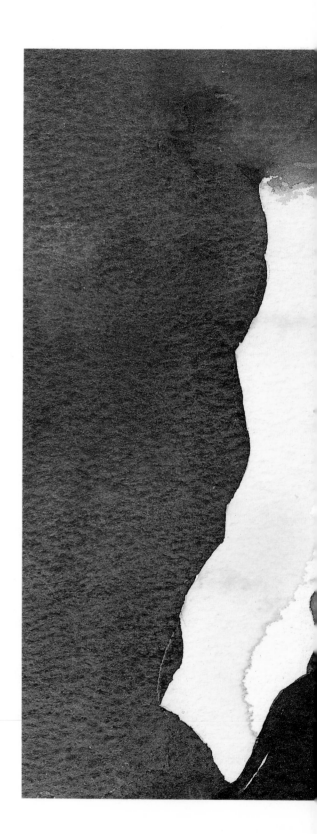

Wu led the horses to the opening and peered inside. The cave opened into a large room where Wu could see the flickering light and wisps of smoke from a campfire. Within he saw two ancient men playing chess on a stone table. One man was dressed in a white robe; the other was in black.

Without speaking, the old man in white smiled and welcomed the boy with a wave of his hand.

Once Wu had settled the horses at the back of the cave, he came to the table to thank his hosts. But the old man in white winked at the young monk and put his finger to his lips to signal silence. Then he beckoned Wu to sit down. On the table was a steaming pot of spiced tea and a large bowl of duck and rice stew.

Wu needed no encouragement. Feeling as though he hadn't eaten in days, he savored every bite of the delicious stew while watching the old men play their game.

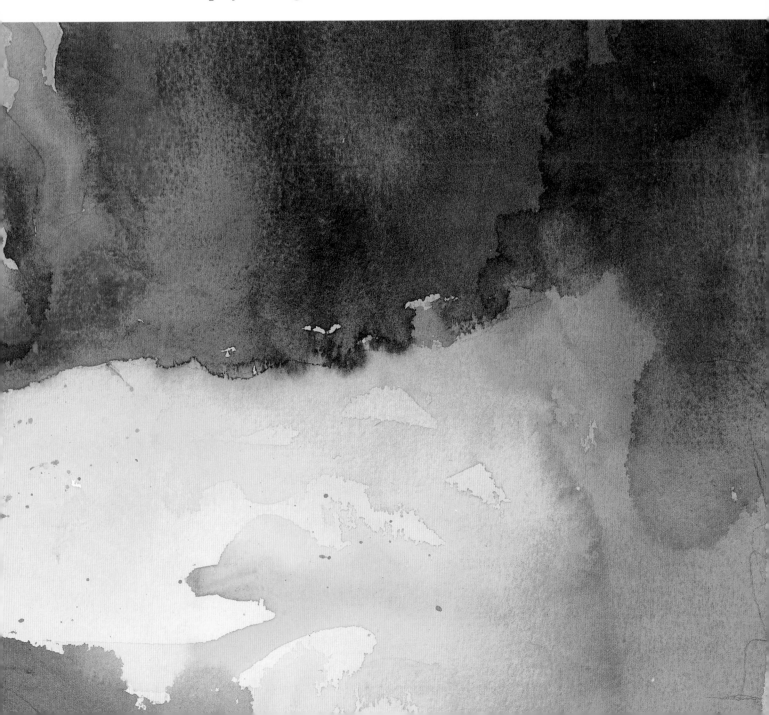

One by one, the chessmen fell. At last only a handful of pieces remained on the board, and the old man commanding the white pieces smiled. He possessed the last pawn.

The white master moved his pawn and the black king was trapped.

The old man in the black robe scowled and pushed his king over to signal his defeat and the end of the game.

The old man in white smiled at Wu and winked again. Reaching across the board, he lifted the winning white pawn and placed it in Wu's hand.

When Wu looked at the chessman, he nearly jumped in astonishment. What sort of magic was this? The tiny pawn was a perfect miniature of Wu!

He suddenly became very frightened. He tried to leap to his feet and flee from the cave, but he couldn't move. He tried to cry out, but could not.

He stared into the strange, yellow eyes of the old man and felt that he could not keep his own eyes open. Had he been drugged by the tea or the stew? Was he under some sort of enchantment? He couldn't fight it any longer. Wu fell into a deep sleep.

When Wu woke up, he felt confused.

He found himself staring at an ivory chessman that lay in his open hand. Suddenly, the memory of all that had happened came back into his mind.

What sort of trick had these spirits played on him?

Wu stood up and walked to the mouth of the cave. Although light streamed in, the cave mouth was sealed off by an enormous, thick curtain of spider web.

Pulling as hard as he could, Wu ripped the web apart and watched it collapse in a dusty heap.

Wu Wing Wong stepped out into the brilliant sunlight.

What a beautiful day, he thought. But as he looked up at the sun, he realized that it was already midmorning, and his next thought was sadly familiar.

"Oh, no! I'm late again!" he shouted.

It was noon by the time Wu made his way with the horses through the woods to the main road. But he found the roads crowded with people fleeing frantically to the mountains.

In the midst of this confusion, Wu came upon two large soldiers on horseback blocking his way.

"I am a monk from the monastery on the Tong Mountains," said Wu. "I must go this way to reach the Emperor's officers by tonight. Please let me pass."

"A monk from the Tong Mountains, indeed!" scowled one soldier, seizing Wu by the collar and pulling him over the saddle in front of him. The second soldier grabbed the packhorses' reins and they all galloped down the road.

As they rode, the terrified Wu saw the country was in turmoil. Soldiers moved in and out of the throngs of people. Farms and houses were burning. The little monk now understood—the people were fleeing from war!

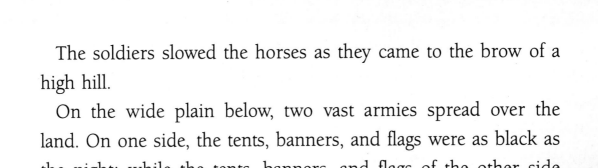

The soldiers slowed the horses as they came to the brow of a high hill.

On the wide plain below, two vast armies spread over the land. On one side, the tents, banners, and flags were as black as the night; while the tents, banners, and flags of the other side were all as white as the snow.

The soldiers rode to a small circle of tents at the edge of the battlefield. Here the banners and tents were the saffron color of his robe, and Wu understood at once that he was in the camp of the monks and priests.

"Father of Priests, please help me," Wu cried to the gray-bearded High Priest of the encampment.

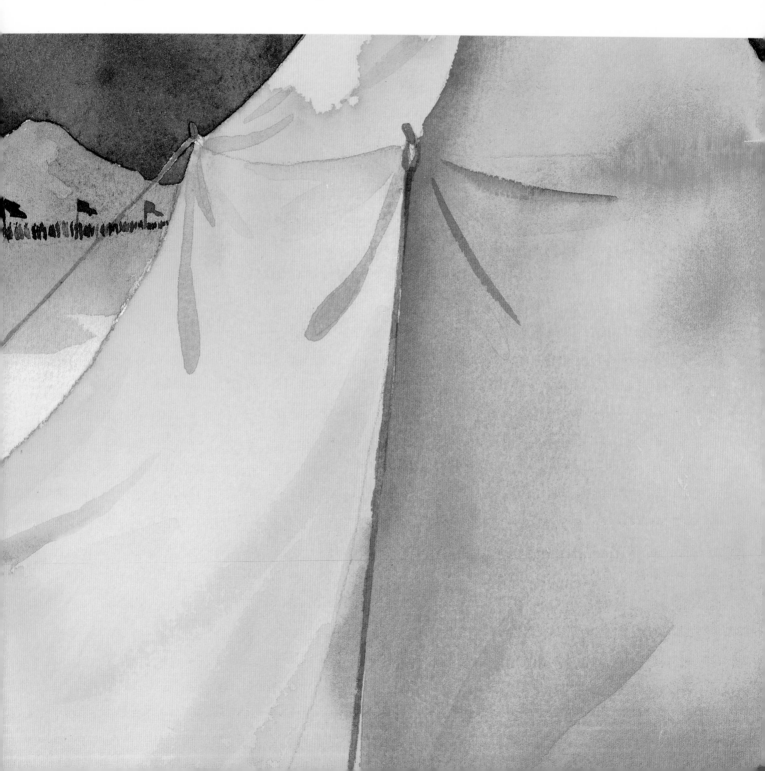

But as Wu told his tale, he could see that the High Priest doubted his every word.

Finally, Wu walked over to the packhorses. Throwing back the covers, he revealed the stacks of books bundled underneath. The High Priest gasped in astonishment.

"I am so sorry, little brother, for doubting your word," the High Priest said softly. "But you must understand that your Emperor Chin has been dead for nearly 200 years, and your great monastery was destroyed by fire over a century ago.

"Don't you see? You didn't sleep on the mountain for one night," explained the old priest. "You slept for 200 years! If it were not for these books, no one would have believed your story."

"I do not understand," Wu said. "What do the books prove?"

"Little Brother, your mad Emperor didn't just hoard the books from the libraries of the Empire. He burned them all!

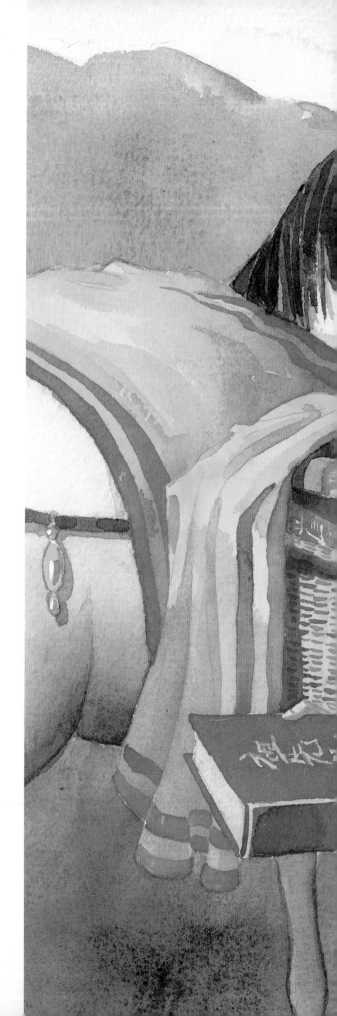

"And since Emperor Chin's reign, China has suffered nearly 200 years of war," the priest continued. "Chin's destruction of the libraries is the cause of the wars. For without the ancient books, it is impossible to prove who should now be the true emperor.

"Tomorrow you will see how the wars continue. The black army of the North and the white army of the South will do battle."

A white army and a black army? Wu could see it was exactly like the chess game in the mountain cave. Suddenly he understood how he was now the decisive pawn in this very real game of war.

Wu searched through the bundles. He soon pulled out a single book—the sacred Book of Ancestors—and he handed it to the High Priest.

The next day, the black army and white army did *not* go into battle.

Wu Wing Wong's Book of Ancestors proved that the White King of the South was the rightful Emperor of China. Even the powerful Black King of the North accepted the authority of the book.

Peace was restored at long last to China. The land prospered again. Wu Wing Wong of Wulung was proclaimed a hero; and soon after, he was made the Imperial Chief Librarian. Slowly books were gathered from far-off lands and new books were written. In time, the shelves in the libraries were filled up again.

But what of Wu's first big problem? As the Imperial Chief Librarian, no one dared to drag Wu from his bed in the morning. He was far too important and was allowed to sleep as late as he liked.

But, in fact, Wu never overslept again. After his 200-year nap in the enchanted cave, Wu found that he no longer needed so much sleep. From that day on, if anyone wished to find Wu Wing Wong of Wulung, they only needed to go to the imperial library at the crack of dawn. There they would find little Wu seated at a table, surrounded by books, happily wide awake and already hard at work.